# LITTLE RED RIDING HOOD
## AND OTHER STORIES

RETOLD BY SUSAN PRICE

ILLUSTRATED BY MOIRA & COLIN MACLEAN

Kingfisher Books

Kingfisher Books, Grisewood & Dempsey Ltd,
Elsley House, 24–30 Great Titchfield Street, London W1P 7AD

First published in 1992 by Kingfisher Books.
2 4 6 8 10 9 7 5 3

The material in this edition was previously published by Kingfisher Books in
*The Kingfisher Treasury of Nursery Stories* (1990).

Text © Susan Price 1990, 1992
Illustrations © Colin and Moira Maclean 1990, 1992

BRITISH LIBRARY CATALOGUING IN PUBLICATION DATA
A catalogue record for this book is available from the British Library

ISBN 0 86272 895 9

Printed and bound in Spain

# CONTENTS

# LITTLE RED

◆ RIDING HOOD ◆

Once upon a time, there was a dark forest, where wolves and bears lived. It was easy to get lost in that forest.

Close to the forest lived a poor woodcutter and his wife. They had one little girl, and they loved her very much. They called her Little Red Riding Hood, because she always wore a hooded cloak that her Granny had made for her. It was as red as poppies or holly berries. Little Red Riding Hood's Granny lived on the other side of the forest.

One day, Little Red Riding Hood's mother put some cakes and bread into a basket and said, "Little Red Riding Hood, take these things through the forest to your Granny. But make sure you keep to the path, so that you don't get lost. And don't stop to talk to *anyone*. Go straight there and come straight back."

"I will," said Little Red Riding Hood.

She set off through the dark forest, in her bright red cloak and hood, carrying the basket.

She hadn't gone very far when she saw some flowers growing by the path. She decided to pick some for her Granny. Then she saw some bigger, prettier flowers growing among the trees, and she left the path to pick them as well.

While she was picking flowers, a wolf came by.

"Good day, Little Red Riding Hood," said the wolf. "How are you?"

Her mother had said not to talk to anyone, but Little Red Riding Hood didn't think a wolf *was* anyone, and so she said, "I'm very well, thank you. How are you?"

"I'm as well as can be expected when I'm so hungry," said the wolf. "That basket looks heavy. Where are you taking it?"

"I'm taking some food to my Granny," said Little Red Riding Hood.

The wolf licked his chops. "If I'm clever," he thought, "I'll be able to eat this little girl *and* her Granny." So he said, "It'll take you a long time to get to your Granny's if you follow that twisty path. I know a shortcut through the trees. Come with me and I'll show you."

"No, I can't come with you, and I'd better go back to the path," said Little Red Riding Hood. "My mother told me not to leave it. You shouldn't *ever* leave the path when you are in the forest. Don't you know that, wolf?"

"Oh, you'll be safe with me," said the wolf. "Come along."

"No," said Little Red Riding Hood, and she went back to the path, with her basket and her flowers.

"Never mind," thought the wolf. "I'll just run ahead to her Granny's and wait for her there."

And off he ran through the trees. Little Red Riding Hood went on her way along the path.

But the way through the trees was shorter, so the wolf reached Granny's house first.

He knocked on the door with his paw. From inside, Granny called, "Who's there?"

The wolf made his voice sweet and soft and gentle, as wolves can when they want to.

"It's your grand-daughter, Little Red Riding Hood, come to see you," he said.

"Then lift up the latch and walk in," Granny called.

But when the door opened, in came the hungry forest wolf, and ate Granny up.

The wolf licked his chops, and dressed himself in Granny's nightdress and nightcap, and climbed into her bed.

He pulled the bedclothes right up to his chin and waited for Little Red Riding Hood.

Little Red Riding Hood came up the forest path to her Granny's house and knocked on the door. From inside came a soft, sweet, gentle voice: "Who's there?"

"It's me, Granny!" said Little Red Riding Hood.

"Then lift up the latch and walk in."

Little Red Riding Hood opened the door and went in.

Little Red Riding Hood stood at the end of Granny's bed and said, "Oh Granny, what big eyes you have!"

"All the better to see you with," said the wolf.

"Oh, but Granny, what big ears you have!"

"All the better to hear you with."

"Oh, but Granny, what big teeth you have!"

"All the better to eat you with!" said the wolf and jumped out of bed. Off fell the nightdress, off fell the nightcap, and Little Red Riding Hood saw that it was not Granny but the wolf! She hit the wolf with her basket and shouted for help as loudly as she could.

Outside in the forest, Little Red Riding Hood's father was at work, chopping wood. He heard Little Red Riding

Hood shouting and ran to see what the matter was. When he opened the door, he saw Little Red Riding Hood fighting with the wolf. With one blow of his axe, he cut off the wolf's head, and out came Granny! She hugged and kissed Little Red Riding Hood, and hugged and kissed her father.

And Little Red Riding Hood never talked to wolves or left the path again.

# THE MAGIC
# PORRIDGE POT

There was once a little girl who lived with her mother. They had no money, and couldn't buy anything to eat. They were hungry all the time.

One day all the mother had to give the little girl for her dinner was one thin biscuit. "Make it last," she said.

The little girl was playing in the street when along came a thin old man. "I haven't tasted a single mouthful in three days," he said. "Can you give me something to eat?"

The little girl gave him her biscuit, because she felt so sorry for him.

"You are kind," said the old man, "and I am going to give you a present." From the pack on his back, he took a little iron pot. "This is a magic pot. It won't work for me, but it will for you. When you want to eat, say 'Little pot, cook!' and it will fill itself with hot porridge. When you've eaten all you want, say 'Little pot, enough!' and it will stop."

The little girl ran home with the pot, and put it on the table. She called her mother and said, "Little pot, cook!"

Straight away the little pot filled with hot porridge, already mixed with milk and sugar. The little girl and her mother ate three bowls each and felt full and happy. Then the little girl said, "Little pot, enough!" and the pot stopped making porridge.

The girl and her mother were never hungry after that.

But one day the little girl was out playing and the mother wanted some porridge. "I won't call her in from her game," she thought. "I know what to say." And she said, "Cook, little pot!"

Nothing happened.

"Oh, wrong way round. Little pot, cook!"

The little pot filled itself with porridge. The mother ate a big bowlful and, while she was eating, the little pot was filling itself again.

The mother didn't want any more, so she said, "Stop, little pot!"

The pot went on filling — and it filled quickly!

"Little pot, stop!"

Porridge began running over the top of the pot.

"Little pot, no more!"

Porridge poured from the pot, over the table, and onto the floor.

"No more, little pot!"

The floor was ankle-deep in gooey porridge.

"Oh what are the right words? Porridge pot, stop!"

Faster and faster came the porridge, rising up the walls,

burying the chairs. The mother opened the door and porridge began running down the street.

"Stop, porridge pot!"

But nothing the mother could think of to say stopped the porridge. It poured down the street and swept a cat off its feet. It ran into other houses and clogged the wheels of cars and bicycles. Porridge everywhere!

The little girl was coming home when she saw a stream of porridge coming towards her carrying along cats and dogs and babies. She guessed what had happened.

She shouted, "Little pot, enough!"

The pot heard her and stopped.

Then everyone had to bring spoons and eat themselves into house and home.

# ◆ THE THREE LITTLE PIGS ◆

Once upon a time there were three little pigs, who set off into the big wide world to make new homes for themselves.

The first little pig was walking along the road when he met a man carrying a load of straw.

"Straw," thought the little pig. "I could easily build a house of straw. It wouldn't take me long, or be much trouble. "

So the first little pig bought the load of straw from the man, and built himself a house with it. And he lived happily in his house of straw.

The second little pig was walking along the road when he met a man carrying a load of sticks.

"Sticks," thought the little pig. "I could easily build a house of sticks. It wouldn't take me long, or be much trouble."

So the second little pig bought the sticks from the man, and built himself a house with them. And he lived happily in his house of sticks.

The third little pig was walking along the road when he met a man with a load of bricks.

"Bricks," thought the little pig. "I could build a house of bricks. It would take a long time, and a lot of trouble, but when it was finished, it would be a good strong house."

So the third little pig bought the bricks from the man, and he set to work to build himself a brick house. It took him many weeks of mixing mortar to stick the bricks together, and of laying the bricks one on top of another to make the walls. Day after day he worked away at it.

The first little pig and the second little pig often came to watch. "Look at you, working so hard!" they said. "We finished our houses long ago, and now we can play."

"Yes," said the third little pig, "but my house will be drier than yours, and warmer and stronger."

But the first little pig and the second little pig didn't think that mattered. They laughed and ran away.

Then came the big bad wolf. Wolves eat little pigs.

The big bad wolf saw the first little pig, and the first little pig saw him.

Away ran the little pig, and shut himself into his house of straw.

"Let me in, little pig, let me in," said the wolf.

"Oh, no, not by the hair of my chinny-chin-chin!" said the little pig. "I won't let you in."

"Then I'll huff, and I'll puff, and I'll blow your house down!" said the wolf.

And the wolf huffed, and he puffed, and he blew down the house of straw. And if the first little pig hadn't been quick, he

would have been eaten. But he was quick, and he ran away to the house of sticks where his brother lived.

The two little pigs shut themselves into the house of sticks, and waited. By and by the wolf came, and the wolf said, "Let me in, little pigs, let me in."

"Oh no, not by the hairs on our chinny-chin-chins we won't let you in," said the two little pigs.

"Then I'll huff, and I'll puff, and I'll blow your house down!" said the wolf.

And he huffed, and he puffed, and he blew down the house of sticks. And if the two little pigs hadn't been quick, they would have been eaten. But they were quick, and they ran away to the house of bricks where their brother lived.

The three little pigs shut themselves into the house of bricks. By and by the wolf came, and said, "Let me in, little pigs, let me in."

"Oh no, not by the hairs on our chinny-chin-chins, we won't let you in," said the three little pigs.

"Then I'll huff, and I'll puff, and I'll blow your house down!" said the wolf.

He huffed, and he puffed – but the house of bricks didn't fall down. So the wolf took a bigger breath, and he huffed harder and puffed harder – but the house of bricks still didn't fall down.

So the wolf took an even deeper breath, and he huffed harder still, and puffed harder still, but the house of bricks just wouldn't fall down, because it was stronger than straw or sticks.

The wolf was exhausted with huffing and puffing, and he crawled away to get his breath back.

The first little pig and the second little pig cheered, because they thought that they were safe now. But the third little pig said, "Help me to fill the cooking pot with water and light a fire under it."

So they lit a fire and they hung the big cooking pot

over it, and they filled the pot with water. The water was soon boiling.

"That wolf won't have given up yet," said the third little pig. "We have to be ready for him."

The wolf got his breath back, and wondered how he could get the little pigs.

He couldn't blow down the brick house because it was too strong. He couldn't get in by the door because it was locked. He couldn't get in by the windows because they were shuttered. But there was the chimney.

So the wolf climbed up onto the roof, and climbed down the chimney to get the three little pigs.

But he landed right in the cooking pot that the three little pigs had ready. So instead of the wolf having pig for his dinner, the three little pigs had wolf stew for theirs.

Then the first little pig and the second little pig built brick houses for themselves, and they all lived happily ever after.

And that's the end of the story.